RETURN TO CREEPE HALL

The further rollicking adventures of Oliver and his weird relatives, the Creepes.

Alan Durant's favourite TV programme, as a child, was *The Munsters*. "I wanted to live in a family like that," he says. "I liked my family and they were interesting, but none of them had green skin or fangs." Several years later, when he was a grown-up author, he decided to write about his childhood fantasy. Hence *Creepe Hall* and now *Return to Creepe Hall*, which introduces a new character, Cleopatra. Alan has written numerous books for young people, including *Jake's Magic*, *The Fantastic Football Fun Book*, *Spider McDrew*, the picture books *Snake Supper*, *Mouse Party*, *Big Fish, Little Fish* and *Angus Rides the Goods Train*, as well as several books for older children. He lives in a fairly ordinary house just south of London with his wife, three young children, cat and a garden shed in which he does all his writing.

Books by the same author

Creepe Hall
The Fantastic Football Fun Book
Jake's Magic
Little Dracula's Fiendishly Funny Joke Book
Spider McDrew
Happy Birthday, Spider McDrew

For younger readers

Angus Rides the Goods Train
Big Fish, Little Fish
Hector Sylvester
Mouse Party
Prince Shufflebottom
Snake Supper

ALAN DURANT

Illustrations by

HUNT EMERSON

WALKER BOOKS
AND SUBSIDIARIES

LONDON • BOSTON • SYDNEY

This one's for Tom Bunker (1987 – 1990)
who, I like to think, might
have enjoyed it.

First published 1997 by Walker Books Ltd
87 Vauxhall Walk, London SE11 5HJ

This edition published 1997

2 4 6 8 10 9 7 5 3 1

Text © 1997 Alan Durant
Illustrations © 1997 Hunt Emerson

The right of Alan Durant to be identified as author
of this work has been asserted by him in accordance with the
Copyright, Designs and Patents Act 1988.

This book has been typeset in Plantin.

Printed in England

British Library Cataloguing in Publication Data
A catalogue record for this book
is available from the British Library.

ISBN 0-7445-5296-6

Contents

Chapter 1

In which Oliver returns to Creepe Hall and hears some exciting news

....

It was great to be back! At last the Christmas holidays had arrived and here was Oliver, standing on the station forecourt in the cool winter air, watching the old black hearse crawl to a halt before him, like a giant beetle. And when the door opened and the driver stepped out, he really was a giant – seven foot tall at least. He raised one hand, so huge it blocked the fading sun, and waved. As he did so, his face was split by a grin that stretched from ear to ear – and what odd ears they were! One massive as an elephant's, the other no larger than Oliver's own. The giant's eyes were equally peculiar – one big as an egg, the other no more than a slit – while his nose resembled a slightly squashed, mouldy carrot. It was a weird sight indeed. Oliver had been quite shocked the first time he'd seen it. But now he smiled.

"Mummy!" he called happily.

"Master Oliver!" the giant thundered in reply, striding stiffly forward. "How absolutely toppin' to see you again, don't you know!"

Mummy wasn't the giant's real name, of course. His real name was Rameses Phaniacus Ozymandias Tutankhamen the Ninth and he was an Ancient Egyptian who had been patched-up and brought back to life by the Creepe family's resident inventor Uncle Franklin. Mummy was Creepe Hall's faithful retainer. Chauffeur, cleaner, cook ... Mummy was all of these, as well as being Uncle Vladimir's assistant in the family undertaking business, which was situated in the funeral parlour behind Creepe Hall.

Once Oliver's trunk was safely stowed in

the back of the hearse, the vehicle rattled into life; just a few minutes later Oliver was reacquainted with Creepe Hall. His feelings on seeing it this time were very different from those on his last visit. Back then his spirits had drooped like a windless sail at the sight of the gloomy old mansion with its sagging roof, broken chimneys and tumbledown tower, and the scruffy wood that bordered it. Now, he viewed these things with deep affection, as if they were old, long-lost friends.

"It's just the same as ever!" he cried ardently.

Mummy chortled loudly. "Oh, my, yes indeed!" he said. "Nothing ever changes at Creepe Hall. It's a world of its own, don't you know."

Of this Oliver was in no doubt. Creepe Hall was certainly not like any place he had ever known – and the Creepes were not like any people he had ever met! They were distant relatives apparently, though what exactly this relation was to him had never really been explained. Not that he cared. He just couldn't wait to see them all again.

As the hearse drew to a halt in front of Creepe Hall something large and black swooped by the window in the gathering gloom. Startled momentarily, Oliver quickly recovered his composure and his smile broadened. It was Uncle Vladimir! He was standing on the steps leading to the front door, a black cloak draped around his shoulders. His lips were drawn back in a grin that revealed two sharp fangs, vampire's fangs – for Uncle Vladimir was indeed a vampire. He often took the form of a bat – especially at night. He had bat-like habits too, such as a tendency to hang upside down from the ceiling, which could, at times, be quite alarming. Right now, though, his expression was warm and welcoming.

"Oliver, my boy! How perfectly splendid to see you," he hissed when Oliver got out of the hearse. Uncle Vladimir's fiery red eyes glowed a little redder as he studied his guest. "You seem rather pink," he tutted. "Never mind, I'm sure we'll soon drain the colour out of you."

Oliver grinned and nodded. The Creepes were all pale. But then that was hardly surprising considering they spent most of their waking lives in darkness. Uncle Vladimir must have got up especially early, Oliver reflected, to welcome him. After all, it was barely twilight.

As Oliver followed Mummy up the grand marble staircase to his room, he was pleased to see that the inside of Creepe Hall was unchanged. It was still riddled with cobwebs and cracks and looked about a million years old – what he could see of it, that was, in the dim light of the candle-lamps. There was no electricity at Creepe Hall, nor was there a television or video, computer or compact disc player. The lack of these things had upset Oliver once, but not any more – who needed a television when you had the Creepes! The place did have some mod cons though. The last time he'd come he'd worked with Uncle Franklin and Cousin Werebadger to produce a few basic household machines – vacuum cleaner, dish-washer, cooker – all powered by Uncle Franklin's solar generator. As he climbed the stairs, Oliver wondered whether any more machines had been added since he'd left.

One piece of machinery that hadn't changed was the large grandfather clock in the hallway. It donged noisily now and made Oliver jump. He glanced back at it from the top of the stairs. Even at that distance he could see that the hands, as ever, were moving backwards. They sort of stuttered too in their movements, like doddery old men. Oliver shook his head. How anyone could tell the proper time from that clock, he did not know. But then no one seemed to bother much about time at Creepe Hall – except for Uncle Vladimir, who insisted on punctuality at dinner. And woe betide anyone who was late!

Having led Oliver to his room and set down the trunk as easily as if it had been a feather pillow, Mummy took his leave.

"Must prepare the dinner, don't you know," he said.

"Oh, yes, of course," said Oliver. "I'll see you in a while."

"Toppin'," declared the giant heartily. "Absolutely toppin'." Then he departed.

Oliver surveyed his room. It was very big, much bigger than his room at home, but also much plainer. There were no pictures on the walls and hardly any furniture. About half of the space was taken up by an enormous four-poster bed, which had thick velvet curtains and was headed by a wood carving of three slightly goofy-looking bats. Opposite, quite high up on the wall, was a gigantic, oval-shaped mirror with a very decorative frame. Standing on tiptoe, he could just about see his reflection in the mirror. On his last visit he'd had to climb up on a chair. But of course, he was six months older now. Soon he'd be eleven. He still had a long way to go, though, to catch up with his cousins. They looked about his age, but were in fact well over a hundred years old! The twins, Constance and Candida, were one hundred and seventy, and their brother, Werebadger, was one hundred and ninety-two!

Happily, Oliver started to unpack his trunk, putting away his clothes in the tall oak wardrobe, whistling as he worked. He was just hanging up his best pair of trousers when the twins walked through the wall! (They were very good at this – and at walking through closed doors too. They could also open locks just by looking at them.)

"What is that dreadful noise!" Candida complained.

"Did someone step on a cat?" suggested Constance. They both stopped still and stared, eyes wide open, dressed exactly the same as always, completely in white – like brides or ghosts.

"Oh, it's you, Oliver!" they cried together,

as they often did when they were excited. "We should have known!" Then they broke into a fit of giggling, which Oliver quickly joined in. How pleased they all were to see each other again! And how much they had to talk about! In no time at all, they were chattering away about old times, recalling Oliver's last visit and the adventures they'd shared. Con and Can told Oliver what had been happening at Creepe Hall in his absence (not much apparently); then Oliver told them what he'd been up to – most of which consisted of details about the battles he'd been having with Damien and Darren, the twins in his class who were always causing trouble.

"Now," said Oliver, "let's go up to the tower room."

The tower room was the cousins' special place. It had belonged to the twins' ancestor, von Batty, but he hadn't been in it for a couple of centuries – not since he'd been caught out in the sunlight and come to an unhappy end. Since then it had been abandoned, until the cousins had discovered it during Oliver's first stay at Creepe Hall. Now the tower room was their den. It was an amazing place too. To reach it, you had to climb up a windy old stone staircase, at the top of which was a creaky wooden door. Open that, as Oliver did now, and you were in a sort of Aladdin's cave of weird and wonderful objects. There was a complete suit of armour, a stuffed bat in a glass case, a wind-up gramophone with a box of records, a chest full of ancient clothes, a huge pair of false fangs and, alongside one of the walls, von Batty's coffin itself.

Oliver wound up the gramophone and put on his favourite record. It was called "The Love Song of the Flea" and it made him laugh. As they listened to the music, taking it in turns to choose a record, the cousins carried on talking and, eventually, the conversation got on to Christmas, because it was now only a few days away. The twins didn't know about Christmas and they wanted Oliver to tell them all about it. They were especially interested in Santa Claus.

"What I want to know," said Constance, putting one long, red fingernail to her chin, "is what kind of beast is this Santa Claws?"

"Yes," agreed Candida. "Are his claws very long?" She waggled her own black fingernails that, like her twin's, were as sharp as an eagle's talons. They did have their use, though – well, the colour of them. For that was the only way that Oliver could tell the twins apart.

"Santa's not a beast at all," said Oliver. "He's a man. And he doesn't have claws."

"Well, why's he called Santa Claws then?" Can said, scraping one fingernail along the lid of von Batty's coffin.

Oliver winced. "I wish you wouldn't do that with your nails," he said. "It sets my teeth on edge."

By way of reply, Can picked up the pair of false fangs and started chattering with them ridiculously. Con giggled and so, a moment later, did Oliver. Soon they were all three in a heap on the floor – and Santa Claus was quite forgotten. They were still laughing when Werebadger burst in.

"Why, Oliver," he said, shaking his cousin's hand with surprising strength for someone who appeared so frail. "It's so g-good to see you again." Oliver grinned. Werebadger was sounding more than ever like Uncle Franklin.

"It's great to see you, too," Oliver said with feeling. The two stood beaming at each other for a moment or two and Oliver took a good look at his cousin. He hadn't changed. Like the others he was wan from lack of sunlight and more bone than flesh, as though he hadn't eaten for a week. Later, of course, he would change totally. When darkness fell and the moon came out, Werebadger would turn from boy to badger...

"So what have you and Uncle Franklin been up to?" Oliver asked. "Made any more amazing inventions?" Werebadger's eyes gleamed. He looked unusually animated.

"Y-yes indeed!" he exclaimed. "Uncle Franklin and I have just made our greatest creation y-yet."

"Brill!" said Oliver. "I can't wait to see. What is it?"

Unlike Oliver, the twins were left cold by Uncle Franklin's inventions. "It's not another of those telly things, is it?" said Can dismissively, balancing the fangs on her nose. Uncle Franklin's attempts at creating a television had not been a success; every picture looked like a vampire in a sandstorm.

"Television, I think you mean," said Werebadger. He shook his head and looked a little forlorn. "N-no, sadly we haven't mastered that as yet."

"What is it, then?" Oliver persisted impatiently.

Werebadger's eyes widened. "Ah, I can't tell you," he said. "It's a surprise – for M-Mummy!"

"A surprise for Mummy!" Oliver repeated

enthusiastically. "Great! When can we see it?"

"Yes, we want to see it!" cried Con and Can together, looking a lot more interested now.

"S-so you c-can," said Werebadger. "Uncle Franklin wants you to come downstairs to the laboratory r-right away. He sent me to f-fetch you."

"Well, what are we waiting for?" said Oliver excitedly and he moved quickly towards the door. Before he could open it, though, the twins passed by him and walked straight through the thick wood. Then they were away down the gloomy old stairwell with Oliver and Werebadger hurrying along behind.

Chapter 2

In which Uncle Franklin's creation is revealed

....

Oliver grinned. Uncle Franklin's laboratory was even more amazing than he had remembered it. He gazed at shelves of test-tubes, glass bottles and jars full of brightly coloured chemicals and potions and goodness knows what. All around the room things buzzed and flashed and bubbled... Everywhere there were wires and cables connected to machinery of all shapes and sizes. His eyes took in the giant mummy case and the human brain in a glass jar. Huge, dusty books were piled high in the corners and looked as though at any moment they might crash to the floor. In the middle of all this, standing before something covered in a white sheet, was Uncle Franklin himself.

"We've come to see your invention, Uncle Franklin!" the twins cried together. "Oliver's here, too!"

Uncle Franklin turned slowly and looked, vaguely, in the twins' direction. "Hello," he said uncertainly. "Who's that?" He peered, frowning, his thick spectacles perched high on his bald head.

"Hi, Uncle Franklin," Oliver said warmly. "It's me, Oliver!"

For an instant, Uncle Franklin's expression remained faintly puzzled, as if the name Oliver was a maths problem whose answer had escaped him. Then his face cracked open in a broad smile.

"Ah, Oliver!" he said. "Oliver, my boy. How excellent to see you... If only I ... could see you. Now, where did I put my glasses?"

"They're on your h-head," Werebadger said helpfully.

"On my head?" queried Uncle Franklin. He reached up and found them. "Why, so they are. What on earth are they doing up there?" He ran one hand over his smooth head and frowned. In the silence that followed it seemed that Uncle Franklin had forgotten all about his invention and about Oliver too.

"We'd love to see what you've made, Uncle Franklin," Oliver prompted.

"Oh yes, please show us!" cried the twins.

"Mmm, yes, what?" muttered the distracted inventor.

"Your invention," Oliver reminded him.

"My invention, ah yes. No, no! My creation!" Uncle Franklin pronounced proudly. "But where is Mummy?"

At that very moment, as if on cue, a giant figure stooped through the open doorway.

"Sorry I'm late!" Mummy boomed in a voice so deep and loud that it made the bottles and flasks rattle. "Had to help Uncle Vladimir with a blighter of an embalmin', don't you know. Hope I haven't missed the big moment."

Oliver didn't know anyone who spoke quite like Mummy. His accent was so rich and upper-class, like a Lord, but a Lord from long ago. It was very weird hearing that plummy voice come out of Mummy's extraordinary face.

"No, no," said Uncle Franklin a little tetchily. "Come along, Mummy. We're waiting for you."

"Oh, absolutely super!" Mummy enthused and he clambered down the staircase. Now it wasn't just the bottles and flasks that shook, but the whole room. It was like an earthquake had started, thought Oliver. (He had heard all about such things from his parents, who'd been in earthquakes several times and were at this present moment up a volcano somewhere in South America.)

At last everyone was ready. They stood with baited breath as Uncle Franklin and Werebadger each took a corner of the white sheet.

"I present my newest and greatest

creation," said Uncle Franklin grandly, then he and Werebadger threw back the sheet. "Meet ... Cleopatra!"

Oliver was used to surprises. Creepe Hall was full of them. But even so, he wasn't prepared for Cleopatra. She was short, not a lot taller than Oliver, and almost as wide as she was high. Her skin was green, like Mummy's, and her features were equally striking. Her hair was bright purple; one eye was as blue as water and one as brown as mud; her nose was bumpy like a boxer's; her ears like two nibbled cabbage leaves and her mouth as round and red as a postbox. But by far the most startling aspect of Cleopatra's appearance was her arms – she had four of them!

"Well, Mummy," said Uncle Franklin. "What do you think of your new workmate, hmm?"

Mummy's response was dramatic. His slit eye suddenly popped out from between its lids like a giant pea from a pod, while the

open eye bulged like a snooker ball.

"Absolutely top hole, don't you know," Mummy enthused. "A ravishin' beauty and no mistakin'!"

Oliver stared at Mummy in disbelief and then looked again at Cleopatra. "She's got four arms," he said incredulously.

"Yes, yes, indeed," said Uncle Franklin. "That was Werebadger's idea. And an excellent one it was too."

Werebadger beamed from ear to ear. "It's so that she c-can be more u-useful to Mummy," he explained.

"Capital! Capital!" Mummy exclaimed. "Four arms are better than two, don't you know."

Actually, Oliver didn't know this – or at least he'd never thought about it before. But he had to admit that it did make sense. Uncle Vladimir was a very demanding master and worked his giant servant extremely hard both around the house and at the funeral parlour. Mummy needed help – and an assistant with two pairs of hands, well, that really would be helpful. A "ravishing beauty" though? No, *that* Cleopatra was not.

"Now, would you like to see her walk and talk?" asked Uncle Franklin. "She does it very nicely, you know."

"Oh, yes, please," said Candida, and she and Constance giggled. Cleopatra was the funniest thing they had seen since they first set eyes on Oliver.

"Werebadger, the lever, if you please," Uncle Franklin instructed.

"Y-yes, Uncle," said Werebadger. Eagerly he went over to the control panel beside Cleopatra and put his hand on the largest lever. With an "oof", he pulled it down as far as it would go. There was a flash of blue light above Cleopatra's head and a thick, smoky smell like after a firework has exploded.

For a second afterwards, nothing happened. Then everything happened all at once. Cleopatra's four arms waggled up and down and sideways and she started to walk ...

backwards. Then she spoke. Well, at least what came out of her mouth sounded like words but it was impossible to make out what they were because of the strangeness of her voice. It sounded like the squeaky noise that comes from a wet window when you rub your finger over it.

"Oh, d-dear," Werebadger sighed as Cleopatra came to a crashing halt, toppling over backwards onto one of Uncle Franklin's work tables. For a few moments she lay there with her arms wiggling frantically like an overturned turtle's, then, all of a sudden, she went completely still, limbs held out stiffly above her.

The twins howled with laughter while Werebadger looked as though at any second he might cry. No one knew quite what to say.

"I think perhaps one or two minor adjustments are in order," Uncle Franklin remarked finally. "These things do take time, you know."

"Oh, absolutely!" Mummy thundered.

"Yes, of course," Oliver agreed, recalling that he hadn't yet put together the radio-controlled aeroplane model he'd been given for his last birthday, and making a human being (if you could call Cleopatra human) had to be much more difficult than that.

"The problem is getting the parts," Uncle Franklin complained to no one in particular. "Now, two hundred years ago, when I re-created you, Mummy, the whole thing was really much more satisfactory. It's this cremation business that's done it..." For the next five minutes or so Uncle Franklin bemoaned the loss of his vital materials. He just could not comprehend why people would choose to have their bodies burnt when they died rather than allowing them to be recycled.

"Thank goodness I saved Alfred," said Uncle Franklin, nodding at the brain in the glass jar. "He was a quite brilliant scientist, you know, quite brilliant. They don't make brains like that anymore, you know."

"Oh quite, indeed," Mummy agreed. "In my day, civilization was much more advanced, don't you know. Why, the art of pyramid makin' has quite vanished. I believe..." Mummy's lecture on the superior brainpower of the Ancient Egyptians was brought to a sudden halt by a loud snuffling noise.

Turning round, Oliver jumped back in amazement.

"Oh!" he cried. He was looking at the black and white striped form of a badger on top of which was his cousin's head, growing longer and furrier by the moment! It was Werebadger making his nightly change. Oliver had seen this process often enough before but the speed of it now took him by surprise. He'd only been at Creepe Hall an hour or so and wasn't quite settled. Things like boys turning into badgers at the drop of a hat didn't happen in the outside world.

Werebadger, entirely badger now, snuffled again and waved his front paws at Uncle

Franklin as if trying to attract the inventor's attention. Uncle Franklin, however, was in a world of his own. His face had gone completely blank and he was running his hand over his bald egghead as if feeling for any bumps or cracks in the smooth dome. Oliver recognized the pose and what it meant – Uncle Franklin's mind was no longer with them; it had moved on to something else entirely and they might as well all leave. He was just about to suggest this when Mummy spoke.

"Goodness!" he cried, his voice like an exploding bomb. "We shall be late for dinner! Oliver, dear boy, you must get changed at once." It was one of the customs of Creepe Hall that everyone had to dress for dinner. Oliver had to wear a suit and bow-tie that, in his opinion, made him look like a stuffed penguin.

"We'll help you get ready," said Con helpfully.

"Oh, yes!" said Can. And before Oliver could say a word, his cousins had each grabbed an arm and frogmarched him swiftly across the room and up the laboratory stairs, with Werebadger bounding after them.

Chapter 3

In which Oliver learns of Uncle Vladimir's woes

....

Dinner that first night was a strange event. It started well enough. Everyone arrived on time and took their places around the huge bat-shaped table. As usual, Uncle Vladimir sat at the head and Uncle Franklin on his own in the gloom at the other end. Oliver sat between the twins. Opposite him Werebadger perched on his seat with his paws and head resting on the table. It was an odd sight that grew even more curious when the soup was served. As the others picked up their fine silver spoons, Werebadger simply stuck his snout in his bowl and emptied it in one loud slurp and gurgle. It was all Oliver could do not to giggle. He didn't, because he thought Uncle Vladimir might not be amused – he took his dinner very seriously.

Uncle Vladimir seemed in very good spirits. He talked to Oliver about the book on bats he'd given to him last time as a leaving present. Oliver said how much he'd enjoyed it, drawing from his uncle a typically toothy grin.

"Ah, excellent, excellent," Uncle Vladimir declared. "There's nothing like getting your fangs into a good book."

"No, no," Oliver agreed. Looking at Uncle Vladimir's fangs, Oliver couldn't help thinking that they could do with a good scrub. In the shadowy light of the candelabra, they seemed particularly dingy.

It was just after Mummy had served the main course – some sort of steak dish – that the atmosphere suddenly changed. They were all eating quite happily, when Uncle Vladimir threw down his napkin and leapt to his feet.

"I cannot eat this!" he stormed, eyes

flashing. "It's been cooked. You know I like my food rare, Mummy, so that I can taste the blood." He pointed accusingly at the food on the plate before him. "This is quite bloodless. And too tough. I ... *ooooh!*" He howled and grimaced as if in great pain and then, like an angry bat, flew from the room, leaving a shocked silence behind him.

Oliver glanced round the table. Werebadger snuffled nervously, a tangle of worms dangling from his mouth. The twins looked paler than ever, almost transparent. Poor Mummy appeared utterly distraught. Only Uncle Franklin was oblivious to what had happened. He carried on eating, at the far end of the table, thinking about Cleopatra, no doubt. No one, it seemed, had anything to say.

"Whatever's the matter with Uncle Vladimir?" Oliver asked at last.

Can shrugged. "That's Papa for you," she said.

"He's very particular about his food," said

Con, pushing her plate away. "Vampires are like that, you know." Werebadger gulped noisily and the worms vanished into his deep mouth. "Werebadgers too," she added.

"But there must be more to it than that," Oliver insisted. Uncle Vladimir did have a sharp temper and could be very fierce, but Oliver had never seen him so angry about something so minor. "He sounded like he was in real pain," he said. But the twins had nothing more to offer on the subject. It was typical of them, thought Oliver, not to know what was going on. He'd ask Mummy. But the giant servant was nowhere to be seen.

"Where's Mummy?" Oliver asked. Con and Can looked at him blankly. Werebadger snuffled insistently and waved his paws. He seemed to be trying to say something.

"Werebadger says he thinks Mummy's gone to see if he can help Papa," Can interpreted. "Personally I think he should stay well away."

"Yes," Can said. She shuddered. "There's nothing worse than an angry vampire."

Werebadger nodded his striped head in solemn agreement.

It wasn't until the next morning that Oliver caught up with Mummy. He found him polishing the old clock in the hall and questioned him about Uncle Vladimir.

"Oh, yes, indeed, things are rather difficult at the moment, don't you know," Mummy said with a deep sigh that sent a whirlwind of dust flying up to the ceiling. "The master is quite out of sorts. What with the bally body-snatchers and this terrible toothache he's sufferin' – life at Creepe Hall is in a pretty pickle and no mistakin'."

"Body-snatchers?" Oliver queried, intrigued.

"Yes, yes," said Mummy. "The bounders have paid us a visit three times now, always on nights of a full moon. Breakin' into the funeral parlour and stealin'. Why, it's an absolute disgrace, don't you know."

"But who are these body-snatchers? What

do they steal?"

"They steal bodies, of course," Mummy said with deep indignation. "Our customers' bodies, the thievin' scoundrels."

"But who on earth would want to steal a dead body?" Oliver persisted in amazement. "And why?"

"They sell them to those medical chappies," Mummy explained. "For research, don't you know. Uncle Vladimir is livid. His professional reputation as a mortician is at stake. If he ever catches the blighters, he says, he'll..." But what Uncle Vladimir threatened to do to the body-snatchers was lost in the loud donging of the grandfather clock. It chimed eleven times, though Oliver was sure it couldn't be any later than nine o'clock. The sun had barely risen.

For the rest of the morning, Oliver's thoughts were completely preoccupied with the body-snatchers. He recalled how cross he'd been a few weeks back when one of the twins in his class, Damien and Darren (he didn't know which, because it was impossible to tell them apart), had taken his hologram ruler. But imagine if someone stole your body, he thought; imagine how angry you'd be then. Except you wouldn't, because you'd be dead, of course. Still...

In Oliver's honour, the twins got up especially early, appearing from their coffin-beds soon after lunch. They and Werebadger joined Oliver up in the tower room and immediately he started talking about the body-snatchers. In fact, he wouldn't talk about anything else. Con and Can started to get quite impatient with him.

"Oh, do shut up about these body-snitchers," said Con. "Let's play cards." She picked up an ancient pack of playing cards and began to shuffle it. "Bite Your Neighbours?" she suggested.

"Oh, yes," said Can. She pointed one sharp talon at Oliver. "And you can tell us some more about Christmas."

"And Santa Claus," said Con. "He sounds

funny. I want to hear more about him."

"Y-yes," Werebadger agreed. "I think that would be m-most interesting."

Oliver abandoned the body-snatchers and did as he was asked. He told his cousins about Santa Claus and his reindeer and the sleigh piled with presents; about stockings and pillowcases and chimneys; about Christmas trees and carols, Christmas pudding and mince pies and snow...

"Snow?" queried Con. "What's snow?"

"Snow, you know!" said Oliver. "Cold white stuff that falls out of the sky. Looks a bit like soap powder. You make snowballs and snowmen out of it."

"Soap powder?" said Can.

"Snowballs?" said Con.

"S-snowmen?" said Werebadger.

"You must know what snow is," said Oliver. Then looking round at his cousins' blank expressions, he added, uncertainly, "Don't you?"

"We haven't the faintest idea what you're

talking about," said Can.

"Is this one of your jokes, Oliver?" said Con.

"I th-think I h-heard Uncle Franklin m-mention it once. It sounds f-fascinating," said Werebadger.

"Well, I don't know about fascinating," said Oliver, "but it's not a joke, it's real. And it's great fun. We had a mega snowball fight at school last year. It was brill. Everyone joined in – even the teachers. I chucked a snowball right down Mr Gummer's neck." Oliver grinned at the memory.

"Did it hurt him?" asked Con.

"Oh no," said Oliver. "It just made him cold and wet."

"Yuck," said Can, who hated getting wet, though she, like all the Creepes, was fond of the cold. Creepe Hall had no heating and was just about the coldest place Oliver had ever been in. Luckily, he'd come prepared this time with lots of warm clothing.

"I m-must tell Uncle Franklin about this

s-snow," said Werebadger.

"I'll come with you," said Oliver eagerly.

Can yawned and, an instant later, Con yawned too.

"We're going back to bed," said Can.

"Yes," said Con. "We shouldn't have got up so early."

By now it couldn't have been later than about half past three, thought Oliver. The pale wintry sun was still peeping in the windows, casting light shadows around the room. But the twins were used to sleeping until sunset.

"OK," he said. "We'll see you later. Sleep well."

Uncle Franklin was delighted to see Oliver and Werebadger. He listened with great interest to what Oliver told him about snow.

"Mmm," he murmured thoughtfully. "I have read something of this snow, but I've never seen it myself. Lightning storms and thunder are common around here, but snow is quite unheard of. I suppose our climate is simply too warm."

"Too warm?" Oliver repeated incredulously.

"Yes," said Uncle Franklin. "I'm sure it was much colder in the old days. But, then, everything was better then..." Uncle Franklin's words tailed off and he stood looking into space as if he could see the past there. Then he ran his hand across his bald dome and frowned.

"Now, what was I talking about?" he pondered, but before either Oliver or Werebadger could say "snow," he continued on another subject entirely – Cleopatra. He wanted to show them the modifications he'd made to his new creation.

"You will find her very changed," he said with a confident air. "I believe that now she should be quite perfect." Oliver looked doubtfully at Cleopatra. He couldn't see any difference in her appearance. She still looked totally weird. However, he kept this thought to himself.

"Just stand there, my boy, and observe," said Uncle Franklin. "Now, Werebadger, the lever, please." As before, Werebadger pulled down the lever and there was the same blue flash and burning smell. What happened next, though, was quite unexpected.

Cleopatra's round red lips formed an exaggerated pout and her thin eyebrows rose and arched into two astonishing bows. Then with a peculiar kind of wiggling movement she walked across to Oliver, put two arms round his waist and two round his neck, lifted him and kissed him full on the lips.

"My," she said in a deep husky voice. "What a big boy you are. And so handsome. Where have you been all my life?"

"Er, ah, Uncle Franklin!" Oliver spluttered, struggling to release himself from the creature's python-like embrace.

"Mmm, yes," Uncle Franklin murmured, rubbing his hand across his smooth chin. "Not quite perfect yet perhaps..."

Chapter 4

In which Oliver solves a teething problem

....

There was no doubt about it – something was seriously wrong with Uncle Vladimir. He was hardly to be seen in the next couple of days, and when he was it was to complain. He complained about the food, the noise the cousins were making, the cobwebs in the hallway (there weren't enough of them!) – everything. In the end he retired to his tomb and said he did not want to be disturbed. He didn't even come out for dinner.

"Are you sure this isn't to do with me?" Oliver wondered anxiously.

"No, no," Mummy assured him. "It's the toothache, don't you know. It's troublin' him somethin' shockin'."

"He should see a dentist," said Oliver. "They're very good these days, you know. It really doesn't hurt at all." This was the very same thing that Oliver's mother had said to him in the dentist's surgery just a few days before he'd come to Creepe Hall. It hadn't convinced him and, even though he repeated it with great confidence, it didn't convince Mummy either.

"Alas, Master Oliver," he said gravely, "I fear that Mister Vladimir would rather die again than go to the dentist's, don't you know. The only strangers he can abide are dead ones."

"Well," said Oliver firmly, "it's plain for anyone to see that those fangs of his are completely rotten and ought to come out. He doesn't use them any more, so what's the problem?"

Mummy frowned and shook his huge head. "Ah, Master Oliver, you do not understand. It is true that Mister Vladimir is not strictly speakin' a practisin' vampire. But the fangs of a vampire, even a vampire who does not bite, are his most prized possessions, don't you know. Why, who ever heard of a vampire without them?"

"Mmm, I see what you mean," Oliver conceded. "But still, if they're giving him that much pain..."

As if on cue, at that very moment an awful cry howled through the big old house, followed by a second that was, if anything, even more pitiful. Con and Can suddenly appeared out of the wall.

"Is there a wolf in the house?" asked Con sleepily.

"Can you please put it out, Mummy?" said Can. "We can't sleep with that racket going on."

"It's not a wolf," Oliver said. "It's your father. He's in terrible pain."

"That's no reason for him to keep us awake," said Can grumpily. "It's not our fault."

"We didn't do anything," Con added.

Oliver looked hard at the twins and pursed his lips determinedly. "No," he said, "you didn't. But it's about time someone did."

Just as the body-snatchers had preoccupied Oliver a couple of days before, now it was the turn of Uncle Vladimir's toothache. He felt very sorry for his uncle, of whom he was really quite fond. It was, after all, Uncle Vladimir who had invited him to return to Creepe Hall. The least he could do now was to relieve his host's agony. But how?

The obvious person to ask for help was Uncle Franklin. He, surely, would be able to come up with some potion or contraption to cure Uncle Vladimir's toothache. The problem was that if Oliver went into the laboratory, Uncle Franklin would insist on his witnessing another Cleopatra demonstration and he really didn't fancy having to face that weird creature again – not until he was sure she was safe. She'd nearly squeezed the life out of him last time.

And then it struck him. Of course! He

couldn't ask Uncle Franklin, but he could ask Werebadger. His cousin was much more practical than Uncle Franklin anyway. He was the one to sort out this problem, he thought.

And, as it turned out, he was right.

Werebadger saw the answer at once. He agreed with Oliver that the rotten teeth really ought to come out. Apart from anything, they smelled so disgusting – even to a badger.

"I b-believe I have just the th-thing," said Werebadger cheerfully and he slipped away to the laboratory, returning to the tower room a few minutes later with what looked to Oliver like a giant pair of pliers.

"Wow!" said Oliver.

"Uncle F-Franklin's extractors," Werebadger informed his cousin. "He uses them for removing brains. I th-think they should d-do."

Oliver looked doubtfully at the enormous instrument. "Maybe," he said. "But they're so big. None of us could use them."

"M-Mummy could," said Werebadger.

"Oh, yes," Oliver agreed. And so it was decided. They would do the deed that very evening, when the twins were up.

So it was at seven o'clock that Oliver, Constance, Candida, Werebadger and Mummy gathered in the dark corridor outside Uncle Vladimir's tomb.

"Are you sure this is right?" Mummy asked anxiously. "I wouldn't like the master gettin' more agitated, don't you know."

"If that tooth doesn't come out," said Oliver, "Uncle Vladimir's mood is going to get much, much worse."

"Oh, dear," said Mummy. "We'd better go ahead then."

"Come on," urged the twins impatiently. Oliver hesitated with his hand on the door handle for an instant, then he turned it and pushed the door open.

As the five figures crept quietly into the

room, they were met by a dreadful wailing and moaning. Uncle Vladimir looked awful, his face was almost as green as Mummy's and his usually ice-cold skin was damp with sweat. He lay in his coffin, tossing and turning, barely conscious. His mouth was wide open, revealing the rotten fangs as clear as day. The stench was quite revolting. Oliver coughed and put his hand over his nose.

"He's bot a bever," Oliver said, behind his hand. "I think be bot here bust in time. Quick, Mummy, be'll hold him down, bhile you use the extractors."

The cousins took up their places on either side of Uncle Vladimir's coffin, two at each end. Then, at Oliver's nod, they pushed down on the patient. At that instant, Uncle Vladimir's eyes blazed open and Oliver feared that their whole mission might be ruined. He and his cousins would not let up their grip, though.

"What the devil..." Uncle Vladimir hissed, but got no further. For at the sight of the

giant extractors approaching him, he fainted.

The first tooth Mummy tried was already a little loose and came out easily. He yanked it free, then held it up for the others to see. It was, without doubt, the most unpleasant thing Oliver had ever set eyes on. Not even Darren's (or was it Damien's?) neck boil could compare with Uncle Vladimir's rotten tooth. The root was all black and bloody and the fang itself was yellow as pus.

"Yuck!" cried Can.

"Eugh!" squealed Con.

"Oh," said Werebadger, who looked at the tooth with some interest, as though considering what use it might be put to in the future. Mummy, meanwhile, had gone quite pale – so pale, in fact, that he appeared almost human.

"Oh, I say!" he exclaimed. "Oh, I say!"

"It's OK, Mummy," Oliver reassured him. "Just one more pull and it'll all be over."

But it wasn't. The second tooth was not half as easy to extract as the first had been.

Mummy tugged and jiggled, pulled and wiggled, but, though the tooth loosened, it would not come free.

"It's no good," said Mummy, with a shake of his giant head.

"The bally thing will not yield, don't you know."

"You'll have to climb up onto the coffin," Oliver told him, "and put your knee on Uncle Vladimir's chest."

"Put my knee on the master's chest!" Mummy boomed in a voice loud enough to wake the dead – but not, fortunately, Uncle Vladmir, who remained as heavily unconscious as a hibernating bear.

"You must," Oliver insisted, adding confidently, "he'll thank you for it, you know," hoping against hope that he was right. The other cousins echoed his instruction and, after a brief hesitation, Mummy complied.

Finally, with a grunt like an Olympic weightlifter, Mummy removed the second tooth. It took such an effort that he toppled backwards and crashed to the floor, tooth and extractors thrown into the air. This time Uncle Vladimir did wake and, at the sight of his disembodied fang flying across the room, promptly fainted once more. When, eventually, he came round again, there was a trickle of blood at the corner of his mouth. He licked at it, then screwed up his long nose in an expression of deep distaste.

"I never could stand the taste of my own blood," he muttered. He looked with some surprise at the five faces staring back at him. His eyes started to glow. Then he opened his now-fangless mouth and grinned.

"The pain – it's gone!" he announced, happily. And, to Oliver, the sight of his uncle's smiling face was like Christmas come early.

Chapter 5

In which Oliver gets a chilly surprise

....

The next morning, when Oliver awoke, he couldn't believe his eyes: his room was full of white foam! I must be dreaming, he thought. He shut his eyes and opened them again, then shook his head vigorously. But it was true! The whole floor was covered in white foam and, he quickly realized with some alarm, lots more of the stuff was seeping in under the door with every passing second. If he didn't get out soon, he thought, he'd be swimming in the stuff. Without another moment's delay, he leapt out of bed.

"Oooh!" he cried. The foam was cold, very cold, as cold as ice-cream! Hopping and ooh-owing, he waded over to the wardrobe and quickly grabbed some clothes and shoes. Then he crossed to the bedroom door and opened it.

The white stuff was everywhere! All along the long corridor it lay like a thick fleecy carpet, and growing thicker by the minute. What on earth could it be? It was sort of like bubble bath, only freezing. Oliver shivered. Creepe Hall was chilly at the best of times, but now it was like a fridge. He shivered again, then set off down the corridor in the direction from which the foam was emerging.

When he reached the marble staircase, he met Werebadger, who'd just picked up a lump of the foamy stuff on his hand and was licking it. From his expression, it obviously didn't taste very nice.

"Eugh!" he spluttered. He started to cough and Oliver patted him firmly on the back.

"What is this stuff?" he asked.

"I-I've n-no idea," Werebadger stuttered. "It t-tastes awful." Oliver reached down and scooped up a little bit of the foam. Then, very gingerly, he touched it with his tongue.

"Yuck!" he said. "It tastes like ... like ... frozen soap!" He noticed something else odd about the foam. It wasn't rising exactly, like you'd expect foam to do; it was sort of creeping up the stairs, as though it were alive. What's more, there was a strong, icy breeze blowing through the air. It was like being outside on a snowy December afternoon.

"There's something weird going on," Oliver said aloud. "We'd better find out where this stuff's coming from before it takes over the whole house and turns us all to ice."

"Y-yes, indeed," agreed Werebadger, his teeth chattering.

The two cousins set off together, holding on to the bannister rail as they climbed carefully down the stairs. They made their way along the hall and into the kitchen.

"L-look!" cried Werebadger, pointing towards the door to Uncle Franklin's laboratory. "It's coming from d-down there!"

Oliver sighed. "We should have known," he

said. "It must be one of Uncle Franklin's crazy experiments. Let's go and see what he's up to."

The noise in the laboratory was terrible. Oliver and Werebadger had to put their hands over their ears. They had to shout, too, really loudly, to attract Uncle Franklin's attention. At last, he heard them and turned off the piece of machinery that was causing all the row. Immediately the breeze dropped and the foam stopped dead on the laboratory stairs. Uncle Franklin was grinning from ear to ear and his bald head glowed pink with pleasure.

"Well," he said. "What do you think? Amazing, eh?" Oliver looked at the machine before him. It was a sort of large metal vat, from which a pipe protruded and below which was a big fan-like thing.

"What is it?" Oliver asked, intrigued. Uncle Franklin frowned, as though the answer to this question was ridiculously obvious. "Why, it's a snow machine, of course!" he exclaimed.

"A snow machine!" cried Oliver.

"Yes, yes, of course," Uncle Franklin reiterated a little tetchily. "What else did you think it might be? A television?"

"No, no, of course not!" said Oliver. "It's just that ... that..."

"Yes?" queried Uncle Franklin. "You said, did you not, that snow was rather like soap powder and that it was cold and covered the ground. Well, there you have it – snow."

For a moment, Oliver was quite at a loss as to what to say. Werebadger came to his rescue.

"I b-believe that snow f-falls from the sky, Uncle Franklin," said Werebadger. "Outside in the open air, n-not inside the house. And it's of a p-powdery consistency, not bubbly. Isn't that s-so, Oliver?"

Oliver nodded. Uncle Franklin ran his hand over his bald head and frowned deeply behind his thick spectacles. "Oh," he said quietly. "Oh, I see."

Oliver felt a little sorry for his uncle, who

seemed to be having rather a lot of disappointments recently with his experiments – in particular the disasters of Cleopatra (who, Oliver was relieved to see, was presently nowhere in sight). He tried to think of something that might cheer him up. "It does feel very cold like snow," was the best he could come up with.

"Ah, that would be the gelatory device," Uncle Franklin muttered. Then he launched into a long and complicated explanation about which Oliver understood nothing at all – but it seemed to cheer his uncle up, so he didn't really care.

"What about all the mess?" he said at last, when Uncle Franklin had finally finished talking.

"Mmm?" said Uncle Franklin. "Mess?" His face assumed a typically vague expression.

"There's foam all through the house," Oliver informed him.

"Upstairs too. Uncle Vladimir will have a

fit if he sees it." To Oliver's surprise, Uncle Franklin had a practical solution for once. He'd just put the machine in reverse, he said, and all the foam would vanish in no time. He and Werebadger would see to it right away. Oliver left them to it and went off in search of Mummy to find out how Uncle Vladimir was faring without his fangs.

He found the giant servant in the kitchen, preparing breakfast.

"The master is somewhat subdued this mornin', I fear," Mummy replied to Oliver's inquiry. "His toothache has quite gone, which is good, but so, of course, have his teeth, which is rather inconvenient for a vampire – especially today."

"Why today especially?" asked Oliver.

Mummy sighed. "Because tonight is a night of a full moon," he said.

Oliver's eyes opened wide. "The body-snatchers!" he cried.

"Precisely," said Mummy. "And Uncle Vladimir is hardly in a fit state to do anythin' about them, don't you know. He can't bite them or fright them without his fangs. I fear he is becomin' sorely agitated again."

"I should have thought he was quite frightening enough even without his fangs," Oliver remarked, thinking of those fierce, burning eyes and recalling how scary he had found Uncle Vladimir when he'd first seen him.

"Well, it's all in the head, don't you know," Mummy said. "Uncle Vladimir just doesn't … feel frightenin'. He needs time to recover – and time, young master, is in terrible short supply. Now, breakfast is served."

Oliver sat down at the table and poured some milk on his cereal. On the floor, the foam was flowing away towards the laboratory, passing under the door, as if being sucked by a giant vacuum cleaner. Oliver watched for a moment or two, then started to eat. As he crunched his cereal he chewed also on Uncle Vladimir's problem.

"But, surely," he said at last, "you could

scare off those body-snatchers, Mummy. I'm
sure they'd be frightened of you." Suddenly
fearing this suggestion might hurt Mummy's
feelings, he added, "I mean, because you're
so big." Mummy started so violently that he
dropped the egg he was holding. It bounced
and broke on the floor, splattering its yoke.

"Me! Scare the body-snatchers!" he cried.
"Oh goodness gracious, no! No! I couldn't
possibly. It's not in my nature, don't you
know."

"But, Mummy, you wouldn't have to do
anything. Just show your face," Oliver
persisted.

"But they might attack me," Mummy said.
"They might have weapons." This thought
made Mummy's face go greener than ever –
like he'd just scoffed down ten bars of
chocolate and a whole cream cake and was
about to bring it all up again.

Oliver was amazed by the giant's reaction.
"You're not scared, are you, Mummy?" he
asked.

"Naturally I'm scared," Mummy replied. "When one has died once, one is not wild about repeatin' the experience, don't you know."

And this was his last word on the subject. Oliver would just have to find some other solution – though what, he had no idea.

Chapter 6

In which Oliver comes face to face with danger

....

Oliver was no coward. He could look after himself. More than once he'd stood up to Darren and Damien when they'd tried to push him around in the playground. But he was only a boy and the body-snatchers, he was sure, were full-grown men. They could be huge. They'd probably be nasty. They might have weapons. He didn't even know how many of them there were. Without Mummy's or Uncle Vladimir's help, well, it seemed to Oliver that there was nothing to be done: the situation was quite hopeless.

This gloomy view, however, was not shared by the twins that afternoon up in the tower room.

"We'll help," they said together with unexpected excitement.

"We love scaring people," said Can.

"It's our favourite hobby," said Con.

"Whoooooo!" wailed Can and she rolled her eyes up out of sight and drew her lips back in a hideous grin. Con followed suit.

"Ugh," said Oliver. "That's horrible. You look worse than Mummy. No, worse than Cleopatra!" The twins giggled.

"What do you expect," said Can airily. "We've been practising for over a hundred and fifty years."

"Yes," said Con. "We can do lots of scary faces. Watch."

For the next ten minutes or so, they treated Oliver to a selection of their most ghastly faces. And they were indeed truly gruesome. There was one, when they seemed to make their faces go inside out, that made Oliver feel quite ill.

"Well, that's all very good," he said finally. "But will it scare off the body-snatchers?"

"We've frightened lots of villagers in the woods," said Con.

"Yes, lots and lots," Can agreed.

"Hmmm," said Oliver. "What we really need is a plan."

"D-did someone say a plan?" asked Werebadger, appearing suddenly in the room. His pleasant face wore an expression of eager anticipation.

"Yes, I did," said Oliver. "And I think you're just the person to help us think one up, cousin." Werebadger beamed rapturously.

"W-with pleasure, Oliver," he said.

The four cousins spent the whole afternoon planning and scheming, discussing and arguing. At last, they came up with an idea that they thought might work. Well, the twins were sure it would; Oliver just crossed his fingers and hoped.

That night the moon was as full as full could be. It hung round and bright as the sun above Uncle Vladimir's funeral parlour behind

Creepe Hall. Inside, the cousins prepared for their unwelcome visitors. Oliver was sitting in an open coffin squinting in the gloom. He was surrounded by other coffins of all shapes and sizes and materials. There was one of black marble that he thought particularly striking. It was Uncle Vladimir's own, the twins informed him. He used it in the summer when the sun became too bright and he needed to take a cool nap.

Mummy had assured Oliver that all the coffins were empty, but even so, he shivered. The funeral parlour gave him the creeps. It was full of shadows from the moonlight and it smelled funny too. He was feeling very anxious.

"Now, let's go over this again," he said. "Werebadger, you go outside and keep watch and warn us when the body-snatchers are coming. Then Con and Can will go outside and I'll lie down in this coffin. When the body-snatchers approach me, I'll sit bolt upright and cry out and that's the twins' cue to walk back in through the wall, wailing." He peered at the twins uncertainly. "You will remember to appear as soon as I sit up, won't you?" he said.

"Of course we will," said Can.

"Relax, Oliver," said Con. "You just lie there and take it easy. Go to sleep, if you like."

"Go to sleep!" exclaimed Oliver. "I can't go to sleep in a coffin!"

"Whyever not?" said Con. "We do all the time."

"Yes, well, you're ... you're..." Oliver struggled to find the right word.

"Yes?" said Can.

"You're ... different," Oliver said. "Anyway, I'm much too nervous to sleep. I wish these body-snatchers would hurry up and come." What he was really thinking, though, was that he'd be very glad if the body-snatchers didn't turn up at all.

"Don't worry, Oliver," said Con. "We'll scare those body-snatchers away."

"And if there's any problem," said Can, "Werebadger can bare his teeth and look fierce. Can't you, brother?" Werebadger, now in his animal form, peered up at his sister and snuffled with a look that was about as fierce as a bag of sugar. Then he bounded off to take up his post outside.

Oliver sighed. "I think Werebadger ought to keep out of sight unless absolutely necessary," he said. "These body-snatchers might be armed."

"Well, I should think so," said Can.

"Yes," said Con. "They'd be funny-looking people if they didn't have arms." And she and Can giggled.

"I'm glad you two think it's all so amusing," Oliver remarked a little testily. An owl hooted loudly from somewhere close by and Oliver almost leapt out of the coffin. "Wh-what was that!" he cried. The twins laughed again.

"You are funny, Oliver," they said through their chuckles.

Then there was another noise, an urgent snuffling in the doorway. It was Werebadger. He was pointing his paw back towards the woods. The four cousins each held their breath and listened. In the silence of the funeral parlour, they could clearly hear footsteps and voices approaching. For a second or two, Oliver froze completely. Then he shook himself into action.

"Quick, everyone! To your places!" he commanded. Then he lay down in the coffin. He was supposed to be pretending to be dead but his body wouldn't stop quaking. His teeth were chattering too and he suddenly felt very cold indeed.

The door to the funeral parlour creaked open and a rush of moonlight entered the room. Two giant shadows appeared on the ceiling – one considerably larger than the other. Oliver's first impression was that there were just two body-snatchers, which was something of a relief. One of them, though, seemed to have two heads, which was rather alarming. There were a couple of clicks and two strong beams of torchlight shone through the room, searching, exploring, until they found the open coffin. Through his closed eyes, Oliver could feel the torch beams illuminating his face. He held his breath, froze, hands and feet clenched tight as if he really were dead and rigor mortis had set in.

Heavy footsteps crossed the floor towards him. He sensed figures looming over him, observing. He felt like he was going to burst.

"Well, well, Burke," said a nasty thin voice. "What do you know? They've gift-wrapped one for us. How very thoughtful."

"Yes," said another slobbery sort of voice which then laughed most unpleasantly. It sounded to Oliver rather like something that should have been behind bars in the zoo.

"A very nice specimen too," said the thin voice. "Young. Not a sign of decomposition. Quite unmarked. Shame it's not a girl, though. We'd get a lot more for a girl's brain than a boy's. Boys' brains are so small and so full of nonsense." A bony finger prodded Oliver in the chest and it was all he could do not to cry out – what with that remark about his brain as well. He caught his breath.

"Mmm," the thin voice continued, "still a bit of air in there. Must be a fresh one."

"Ooh yes, a fresh one," the other voice slobbered evilly, as though he were talking about some delicacy on the dinner table. "Let's take it now."

"No time like the present," said the thin voice. "Shall you take the head or shall I?"

Oliver had heard enough. He wasn't going to play dead a moment longer. He sat up, opened his eyes and yelled. There was an awful screech as one of the body-snatchers threw up his arms and cowered away from the coffin. It was the one with two heads – only he didn't have two heads. Oliver could see that now. He had one head and a hunch back. It was the other body-snatcher who was really taking his attention, though. He didn't seem to be scared at all. He stood, staring at

Oliver with a nasty smirk on his skinny lips. His eyes were dark as a snake's and a scar like a bolt of lightning zigzagged down one cheek. He raised one bony finger and pointed at Oliver.

"So," he rasped. "We have company." Behind him the hunchback slobbered and whimpered in the shadows.

"It's a ghost, Hare! The boy's a ghost! Don't you see! Let's get out of here!"

But Hare showed no inclination to leave – quite the reverse. He stood just where he was and laughed. It was a wicked cackle of a laugh and it made Oliver tremble.

"This boy's no more a ghost than you or I, Burke," said Hare. "I knew he was alive the moment I set eyes on him. Corpses don't breathe, you see, and they don't flush either like this one did when I made that remark about his brain." Oliver went very pale.

"Still," Hare continued, "if he wants to be a corpse, that's fine by us. Is it not, Burke?"

"Yes indeed," Burke slobbered, as if he

couldn't wait to get the job done. He reached into a black bag and pulled out a long, sharp knife.

Oliver was terrified. Where on earth were the twins? Why hadn't they appeared? And what about Werebadger? Oliver could do with his strong teeth now. He could do with any help he could get.

"Con! Can! Werebadger!" he croaked, his voice weak from fear. "Werebadger! Con! Can! Come out now! Help!"

Hare laughed again. "Still full of tricks, I see," he said.

"There's no one here but us. No one's going to save you, boy. You might as well lie back and accept what's coming. Your coffin awaits…" He nodded to Burke and the hunchback shuffled forward, the knife clasped in his large fist, ready to plunge down…

"No!" Oliver cried. "No! Help! Help!" He moved to get out of the coffin, but Hare moved faster. His strong bony hands pressed

down on Oliver's shoulders, pinning him back in the coffin. Then Oliver was staring up at the hunchback's hideous, twisted face and his mouth of black and broken teeth; then the knife appeared in front, obscuring everything, coming down towards his heart...

Wham! Crash! The doors to the funeral parlour exploded open and something stamped across the floor. Burke hardly had time to turn halfway before a pair of arms gripped him round the waist and lifted him from the floor, the knife slipping from his hand. Quick as a flash, Hare bent forward to pick it up, but he too was caught in a crushing embrace. Oliver gaped at the two figures twitching and struggling in the grip of the four arms – four arms! Then he caught sight of the purple hair.

"Cleopatra!" he shouted. "Cleopatra!" He never thought he'd be pleased to see Uncle Franklin's crazy creation.

"Hi, big boy!" Cleopatra smooched huskily. "I seem to have my hands full just now. I'll catch you later." With a waggle of her cabbage

ears and a wink of her bright blue eye, she
scuttled away backwards, like a crab, carrying
the helpless body-snatchers in her arms. Then
she was gone.

Chapter 7

In which the festive spirit is sorely lacking

···

"Where on earth were you?" Oliver demanded sharply next morning. "I could have been killed no thanks to you." He was standing at the end of the twins' coffin beds, glaring. The twins looked up at him sleepily.

"Mmm? What?" inquired Can between yawns.

"Last night in the funeral parlour," said Oliver. "You didn't appear. What happened to you?"

"Oh, yes," said Can rubbing her eyes. "That was Werebadger's fault."

"Yes," Con agreed wearily. "It was Werebadger."

"Now, can we go back to sleep, please?"

said Can and she closed her eyes. But Oliver wasn't satisfied.

"No, you can't," he said. "You can tell me exactly what happened. I think I deserve an explanation."

"Ask Con," said Can, without opening her eyes. Oliver gave Con a searching look.

"Well?" he asked.

"Oh, all right," said Con. She yawned and stretched and waggled her red-nailed fingers. "It was like this. We were in our positions ready to appear and be spooky when Werebadger suddenly came bounding up, snuffling and sniffling all excitedly. It seems that he thought he'd seen the ghost of his ancestor – you know, the first Werebadger, who got killed by poachers in the woods. And he – our Werebadger, I mean – insisted that we go with him into the woods to find the other Werebadger. So we did."

"But what about … me?" Oliver insisted. "I was nearly killed, you know."

"Yes," said Con, and she looked unusually

sheepish. "I'm sorry about that, Oliver. You know how upset we'd have been if anything had happened to you. We really would. It's just that, well, we forgot all about the body-snatchers. Sorry." Oliver was quite taken aback. It was the first time he'd ever heard either of the twins say they were sorry about anything. What's more, Con had said it twice ... and she actually looked like she meant it.

"Well, it worked out OK in the end," he said. "Thanks to Cleopatra."

"Yes," said Con. "Good old Cleopatra."

"I suppose I ought to go and thank her," said Oliver.

"Yes, good idea," said Con and she grinned. "Then some of us can get some sleep..."

As Oliver walked along the corridor towards the marble staircase something dark swooped past him. It was Uncle Vladimir. He landed at the top of the stairs and observed Oliver keenly for a moment or two. Then his mouth opened in a toothless smile and his red eyes glowed. He didn't look at all himself, though, Oliver thought.

"Congratulations, my boy," Uncle Vladimir hissed, his voice more lispy than ever now that he'd lost his fangs. "You have saved my reputation."

Oliver blushed. "It wasn't really me," he said. "It was Cleopatra."

"Nevertheless," Uncle Vladimir intoned, "you are a very brave boy – and clever too. That's two problems you've got your teeth into. Why, who knows, you might make a vampire yet." He smiled again, but a little half-heartedly, as though he were trying to put on a brave face and not quite succeeding. Then, gathering his black cloak about him, Uncle Vladimir swooped away again into the gloom.

There was no sign of Cleopatra in the laboratory – and neither Werebadger nor Uncle Franklin had the faintest idea where she was.

"She's j–just v–vanished," said Werebadger. "N–nobody's seen her since she w–walked off with the b–body–snatchers." He looked down at his feet and two spots of pink appeared on his pale cheeks. "I'm v–very s–sorry about l–last night," he said. "It w–was all m–my fault." He looked so crestfallen that even if Oliver had still been feeling cross, he couldn't have said so. But, anyway, after his talk with Con, Oliver was in good spirits.

"It's OK," he reassured his cousin. Then he remembered something his mum often said. "All's well that ends well."

"But it hasn't, has it?" said a testy voice. Oliver glanced across at Uncle Franklin, who was staring at him with unusual attentiveness.

"What do you mean?" Oliver asked, somewhat bewildered.

"I should have thought that was obvious," said Uncle Franklin irritably. "I haven't created snow, have I, mmm?"

Oliver suddenly felt very tired. He'd got to bed really late the night before and with all the tension and excitement of what had taken place, he felt quite drained. So he decided to go back to bed. He slept like a baby and when he woke up again, the light was already fading outside. It was only then that he realized what day it was: Christmas Eve. And with this realization came a feeling of deep sadness. His lip quivered and his throat tightened and before he could help himself, he had started to cry.

It was in this state that the twins found him when they appeared a few minutes later, passing through the wall. They thought that Oliver was upset about what had happened with the body-snatchers, but it wasn't that. He found it difficult to explain just what was the cause of his tears. But he tried.

"It's Christmas Eve, you see," he said weepily, "and tomorrow's Christmas Day. And normally I'd be at home and we'd have decorations and a Christmas tree and lots of presents all wrapped up around it. And we'd sing some carols... I love being at Creepe

Hall; it's the best place in the world. It's just that, well, I love Christmas." He broke down and started sobbing again.

This sort of behaviour was so unlike Oliver that the twins didn't know what to do. They tried changing the subject, but that didn't work, so in the end they tackled the matter head-on and asked Oliver some more questions about Christmas. And it seemed to work. Oliver told them about Christmas customs, about stockings and mince pies and holly. He told them that his parents had promised to buy him a new computer and about some of the other presents he hoped he might get. After a while, he no longer felt like crying. He still felt a little sad, but was much more himself. He even managed a smile.

"I'll be all right in the morning," he said.

That night they all had dinner together for the first time in days. The atmosphere was distinctly subdued, however, and hardly a word was spoken. It wasn't only Oliver who was out of sorts. Uncle Vladimir had dropped any pretence of a brave face and looked as miserable as could be. The lack of his fangs was really getting him down and to see him mashing gummily at his food was a truly pitiful sight.

Meanwhile it was the lack of snow that was preoccupying Uncle Franklin and the lack of Cleopatra that was worrying Werebadger and Mummy.

"I really don't know where the gal could have got to," Mummy sighed when Oliver inquired if the newest member of the household had returned yet. "A beautiful young thing like her shouldn't be out roamin' the countryside alone like this. Who knows what might become of her?" On another occasion Oliver would have challenged Mummy's description of Cleopatra and suggested that if anyone could look after herself, she could – it was those meeting her who needed to watch out – but this evening he was too weary to do anything more than offer a grunt of concern.

The twins could generally be relied upon to boost the conversation at dinnertimes with their lively chatter, but tonight they were unusually quiet and thoughtful. Indeed when Oliver, in a vain attempt to lighten the mood of the table, suggested to Candida that they might play a game of Bite Your Neighbour after dinner, she shrugged unenthusiastically.

"Con and I have got some things to do," she said mysteriously. "Besides, you'll probably be wanting to get to bed early after last night." It was not a statement that pleased Oliver greatly, though he had to admit that he was very tired after the exertions of the night before. When dinner was over, he took Can's hint and departed for bed.

It was without doubt, he decided, the least festive Christmas Eve he had ever spent.

Chapter 8

In which weird and wonderful things occur and Oliver makes a promise

···

It was still dark when Oliver woke next morning. But then he always woke early on Christmas morning – although, as he quickly remembered with a pang of disappointment, this year there wasn't any Christmas. Not for him. He closed his eyes again and stretched out his legs. *Thud!* His feet collided with something solid on top of the bedclothes.

"Hey! Who's that?" he cried, thinking there was someone sitting on the end of his bed. But it wasn't so. There was something there, though – a little mound. He leaned forward and pulled it towards him.

"B-! W-! Oh!" he exclaimed in

astonishment, as he realized what it was he was holding. There, between his slightly trembly hands, was a large and bulging stocking! He could not believe it. Where could it have come from? Who could have put it there? Santa Claus? No, it wasn't possible. Santa at Creepe Hall? That would be incredible ... only, as he had seen so many times already, anything was possible at Creepe Hall. It was, as Mummy was fond of telling him, a world of its own.

A thrilling tingle ran down his spine as he put his hand into the stocking and started to unpack its treasures. And what an odd assortment of treasures they were! There were some black plastic bats on elastic, a chocolate heart, a pair of joke teeth, a book on Ancient Egypt that looked as if it had been handwritten and illustrated, a sarcophagus money box that creaked open to reveal a grinning mummy when you put a coin in... There was even, to Oliver's amusement, a bottle of linseed oil. He'd once told Uncle Vladimir that linseed oil was ideal for rubbing on bats (cricket bats, he'd meant, of course) and later found out that his uncle, getting the wrong end of the stick, had tried it out on himself! At the time it had been very embarrassing, but now even Uncle Vladimir saw the funny side. How amazing, thought Oliver, that he should find a bottle of the stuff in his Christmas stocking. But then, the whole thing was amazing. Not that he was complaining. Right now he was a very happy boy indeed.

He leapt out of bed, eager to share his happiness with his relatives. But first he ran over to the window to let a little more light into the still gloomy room. Joyfully he whisked back the curtains ... and froze! Once again, he could not believe his eyes. He shut them tight, then opened them again. Shut them and opened them. It was extraordinary, but true. The whole landscape, as far as he could see, was white and glistening with snow.

"Wow!" he murmured. "Brill!" He'd never seen snow like it, so bright and thick and even. It was a magnificent sight. He goggled at it in wonder for a moment or two, then he grinned as his mind started to understand its significance. At last, Uncle Franklin had succeeded in creating snow! He must go at once to the laboratory to congratulate him.

Throwing on some clothes, he rushed out of his room, then along the corridor, down the marble stairs, through the corridor, his heart every bit as light and happy as on any other Christmas Day. He crossed the kitchen in a few deer-like bounds and threw back the heavy laboratory door as if it were made of polystyrene.

"Happy Christmas, Uncle!" he cried.

The words died on his lips. The laboratory was dark and still and strangely silent. There was no whirring or clicking or bubbling or squeaking. No sound at all. And no sign of Uncle Franklin. But Uncle Franklin was *always* in his laboratory – the only time he left it was for dinner. He never slept and he didn't eat breakfast – so where was he? Everything was so weird today, thought Oliver. And for an instant he wondered whether it might all be a dream. He pinched himself just to make sure. No, he was awake all right. He'd have to find Mummy. Mummy would know what was going on. He always did.

There was still no sign of life in the kitchen or in the hall. The grandfather clock showed half past eleven, but that wasn't much help, as its hands were still juddering backwards. It was light now – well, as light as it ever got in the winter in Creepe Hall – so Mummy, Oliver was sure, must be up. He was always the first to appear in the morning.

As Oliver stood there in puzzled thought, his attention was taken suddenly by a noise. It sounded like a giggle, a girl's giggle, and it seemed to come from the dining hall. Swiftly, he crossed to the great wooden doors and, putting his hands on the big brass handles, shoved them open…

If he'd been amazed by everything that he'd seen so far that morning, now he was completely and utterly gobsmacked. Nothing could have prepared him for the scene that met his boggling eyes. All around the room were lit candles, decorated with sprigs of holly; colourful paper chains hung across the ceiling, stretching from one corner to another; a glittering silver star dangled from the chandelier above the bat-shaped dining table, which was itself adorned with candles and seasonal arrangements of dark green holly leaves and bright red berries. And there, at the far end of the room, directly in front of him, was the most astonishing and marvellous sight of all: a beautiful, bushy, gigantic Christmas tree, sparkling with tinsel and baubles and topped by another star – a gold one, this time, that shone in the dimness like a torch.

As he stood dumbstruck, figures emerged from the shadowy corners about him.

"Merry Christmas, Oliver!" they cried and it was all Oliver could do not to start blubbing. He felt tears well in his eyes but somehow managed to hold them back. The figures had gathered around him now: Constance and Candida, Werebadger, Uncle Franklin, Uncle Vladimir, Mummy – even Cleopatra was there. She winked at Oliver and made an exaggerated kissing motion with her lips.

"Merry Christmas," said Constance, and she gave Oliver a peck on the cheek. Then Candida did the same.

"Merry Christmas," Oliver replied weakly, the tears rising once more.

"Compliments of the season, don't you know," Mummy rattled. He grabbed hold of Oliver's hand in one of his own enormous mits and shook it so vigorously that Oliver's whole body wobbled and swayed like an electrified jelly.

"M-M-Merry Christmas," said Werebadger, smiling shyly.

"Yes, indeed," agreed Uncle Franklin. "Merry, Merry..." His eyes glazed over and he ran his hand over his bald crown – a sure sign that his mind had wandered. Oliver chuckled.

"Merry Christmas, Uncle Franklin," he said cheerfully. "The snow's brilliant! I can't wait to get outside and feel it." Uncle Franklin's eyes suddenly came back into focus and stared straight at Oliver, his gaze sharp as a needle.

"Snow, snow," he muttered. "Whatever do you mean?"

"You did it," said Oliver. "Look outside. There's snow everywhere. Tons of it."

Uncle Franklin appeared perplexed. "How extraordinary," he said. "How very extraordinary. Now, however could that have happened? I must go and see," and he hurried away.

Uncle Vladimir glided forward. "Merry Christmas, my boy," he hissed, his eyes aglow. He held out one of his long white hands, which Oliver shook, shuddering a little as he did so. Uncle Vladimir's eyes were like fire, but his hands were like ice. Oliver looked up to be met by one of Uncle Vladimir's toothiest grins. He grinned back. Then he frowned. Something was wrong.

"Uncle Vladimir!" he exclaimed. "Your fangs! They're back!"

"Mmm, yes." Uncle Vladimir beamed. "As good as new. But then they *are* new. Werebadger fitted them for me, bright boy." Werebadger blushed, but Oliver could tell he was very pleased.

"I used the f-false f-fangs from the t-tower room," he explained. "They f-fitted perfectly."

"One vampire's fangs are very much like another's," Uncle Vladimir asserted suavely. Then he waggled his jaw about to show how securely the teeth sat in their new setting.

"Brill! You are clever, Werebadger," cried Oliver, happy to divert attention away from himself. All these surprises were quite overwhelming – and there were more to follow.

It was Con and Can, Oliver discovered, who were responsible for organizing all the decorations and the Christmas tree.

"We couldn't bear to see you so unhappy," said Con.

"No," said Can. "It was too awful." Then she pulled the most ridiculously miserable face and Oliver laughed.

"Thank you all very much," he said. "Now, let me show you the snow."

"No," said the twins, speaking as one. "First we've got something to show *you*."

Con, Can and Werebadger led Oliver up to the tower room.

"Tra-la!" sang Can, when they were all inside. "Look what Uncle Franklin and Werebadger have made for you."

"Yes, isn't it brill?" said Con with a wide smirk. Oliver examined this new creation, which appeared to be Alfred, the brain from the laboratory, attached by a number of wires to a kind of television screen.

"Wow!" he uttered. "What is it?"

"It's a c-computer," said Werebadger, sounding a little put out that Oliver hadn't recognized this at once.

"Oh yes, of course it is," Oliver bluffed. "Only, well, it hasn't got a keyboard."

"It d-doesn't need one," Werebadger replied and went on to explain at unusual length how the computer worked – sounding, it seemed to Oliver, uncannily like Uncle Franklin. By the end of this long explanation, Oliver just about gathered that all you needed to do to operate the computer was speak to it.

"Can it play games?" he asked.

"It can d-do anything," said Werebadger. "T-try and see."

So Oliver did. For the next hour or so he tried all sorts of things. He played Attack of the Killer Alien Reptiles and Super Mega Marion Sisters Meet Binbendo Drain Boy. With the help of his cousins, he even invented a couple of new games – Battle of the Evil

Body-Snatchers and The Vampire Strikes Back. It was great fun. As Werebadger had claimed, the computer could do anything. It knew everything too. You could ask it the most bizarre questions and it always came up with the right answer: What is 74 x 95? Where is Lapland? What does BFG stand for? When is a door not a door? The computer flashed up the answers to them all.

"That Alfred must be some brain," said Oliver, deeply impressed.

"He's the b-best," said Werebadger.

"No," said Oliver. He stared at his cousin with affection and admiration. "You're the best..."

One question that Oliver never even thought of asking Alfred was, "Where is the best place in the world?", because he knew, without any doubt, it was Creepe Hall. And this, he was equally certain, was the best Christmas he had ever had. After playing with the computer, the cousins went out into the snow which, Oliver learned, really had nothing to do with Uncle Franklin. It was just another of the wonders on this most wonderful of days – though Uncle Franklin suspected it had something to do with Oliver's presence.

"After all, it's not every day a living mortal visits Creepe Hall," he said with a wide smile.

Together the cousins built a snowmummy and then had a massive snowball fight that even the grown-ups joined in. Cleopatra was particularly enthusiastic. She had finally returned the night before after a day lost in the woods, but seemed no worse for wear from her experience. Indeed, she was full of energy – and lethal too, for with her four hands, she could make one snowball and throw another at the same time!

Cleopatra also proved an invaluable assistant to Mummy in preparing the feast that followed – the highlight of which was a spectacular and enormous Christmas pudding topped by a holly bat with red berry eyes. It was all very festive and everybody was in the best of spirits. To Oliver's great surprise, Uncle Vladimir even sang a song. It was called "The Ballad of the Lonely Vampire" and told the story of a sad vampire who lived all alone in the darkness, until one day he rescued a maiden from an angry mob and took her back to his castle. This song brought the dinner – and the day – to a rousing ending. Everyone clapped and cheered, and then Uncle Franklin stood up and proposed a toast.

"To our special guest and favourite relative, Oliver," he said, raising his glass. In the candlelight his eyes twinkled like baubles behind his thick spectacles. "To you the doors of Creepe Hall shall always be open."

"Here, here," Uncle Vladimir agreed heartily.

"To Oliver," the others echoed warmly. Oliver felt so full of happiness, he feared he might burst. What a day it had been!

Before getting into bed that evening, Oliver stood for a while at his bedroom window, watching the snowflakes fall from the dark sky to the white ground below. Soon, he knew, he would have to leave Creepe Hall and go back to the normal world of home and school. Tonight, though, that world seemed no more than a dream; tonight nothing could spoil his happiness. Nothing.

Besides, as he stood there in the dark, he promised himself that he would return to Creepe Hall at the very first opportunity. And, well, who could tell, maybe one day he might come back to stay in this weird and wonderful place with these weird and wonderful people for ever.

The Ballad of the Lonely Vampire

Long ago in a faraway country,
Where the wolves roamed wild and free
And bats flew thick in the moonlight
As far as the eye could see
Lived a lonely vampire!

His home was an ancient castle,
High on the crest of a hill,
Where he lived by himself in the darkness
And slept in his coffin so chill.
Oh, the lonely vampire!

One night as he sat at dinner,
Alone in his castle keep,
He heard a pitiful howling
That made him want to weep.
Oh, the lonely vampire!

He rose up from his table
And flew to the wood below,
Where he saw a maiden running
And an angry crowd in tow.
Oh, the lonely vampire!

As the baying crowd came closer,
The maiden tripped and fell,
And down swooped the lonely vampire,
Swift as a bat out of Hell.
Oh, the lonely vampire!

Into his arms he took the maid,
Into the sky they did soar,
Far from the wicked cries of the crowd
And safe to his castle door.
Oh, the lonely vampire!

Said the maid, "Kind sir, I thank you,
My champion from above."
Then she kissed the lonely vampire
And his heart was filled with love.
Oh, the lonely vampire!

But, alas, thought the lonely vampire,
When she knows what I am she'll flee,
And I shall be lonelier than ever,
Without this lovely lady.
Oh, the lonely vampire!

But as they stood in the darkness,
The full moon slid from a cloud,
And he saw the maiden grow hairy
And then like a wolf she howled.
Oh, the lonely vampire!

"Oh maid, I see you're a werewolf
And I am a vampire," he said,
"The match could not be more perfect,
Oh, come now, let us be wed."
Oh, the lonely vampire!

And so to a happy conclusion
Comes my moonlight tale of yore,
For once wed, that lonely vampire
Was never lonely more.
Oh, the happy vampire!